The Train They Call the CITY OF NEW ORLEANS

STEVE GOODMAN

illustrated by

MICHAEL McCURDY

G. P. Putnam's Sons · New York

To the memory of my father,
Charles McCurdy (1910–1964),
who purchased my Lionel train set,
which served as the model
for the drawings in this book. —M. M.

"City of New Orleans" words and music © 1970 by Steve Goodman
Jurisdad Music/Turnpike Tom Music (ASCAP)

Illustrations copyright © 2003 by Michael McCurdy
All rights reserved. This book, or parts thereof, may not be reproduced in any
form without permission in writing from the publisher, G. P. Putnam's Sons,
a division of Penguin Putnam Books for Young Readers,
345 Hudson Street, New York, NY 10014.
G. P. Putnam's Sons, Reg. U.S. Pat. & Tm. Off.
Published simultaneously in Canada.
Manufactured in China by South China Printing Co. Ltd.
Designed by Gunta Alexander. Text set in Wilke Bold.
The art was done in scratchboard and watercolor.

Library of Congress Cataloging-in-Publication Data
Goodman, Steve. The train they call the City of New Orleans / Steve Goodman ;
illustrated by Michael McCurdy.   p. cm.
Summary: An illustrated version of the familiar song about riding on a train
called the City of New Orleans. 1. Children's songs—United States—Texts.
[1. Railroads—Songs and music. 2. Songs.] I. McCurdy, Michael, ill. II. Title.
PZ8.3.G6235 Tr   2003   782.42164'0268—dc21 2001050179
ISBN 0-399-23853-0   10 9 8 7 6 5 4 3 2 1 First Impression

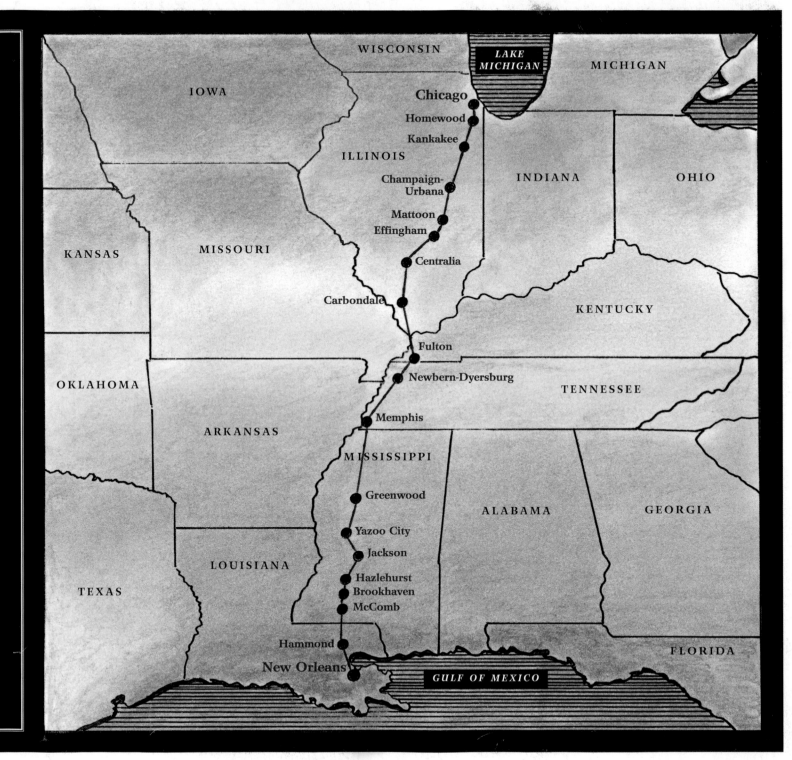

The stops along the journey from Chicago to New Orleans on the **CITY OF NEW ORLEANS**

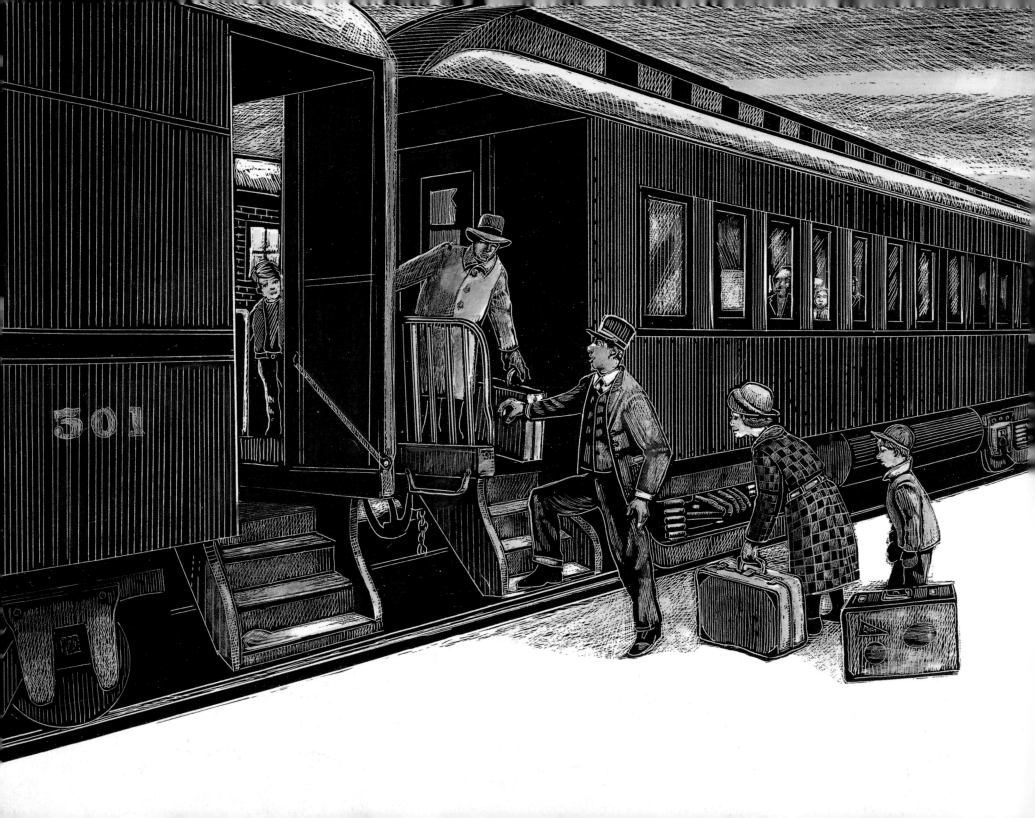

Riding on the City of New Orleans
Illinois Central Monday morning rail

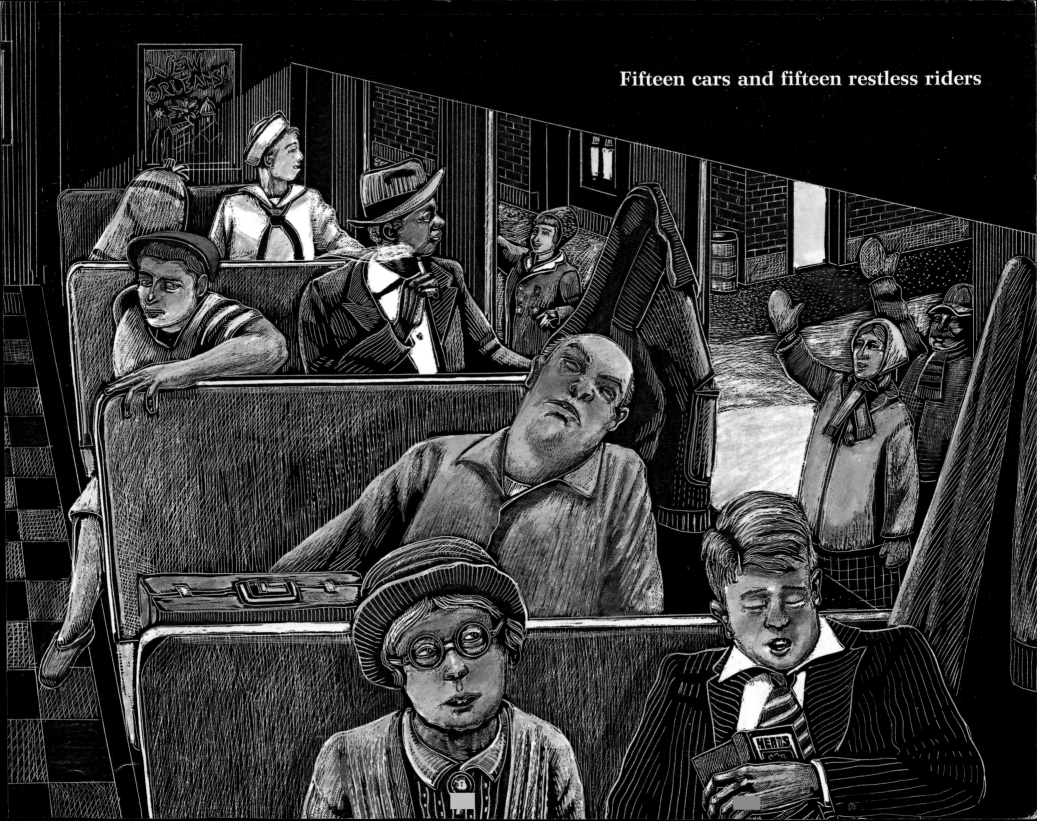

Three conductors,

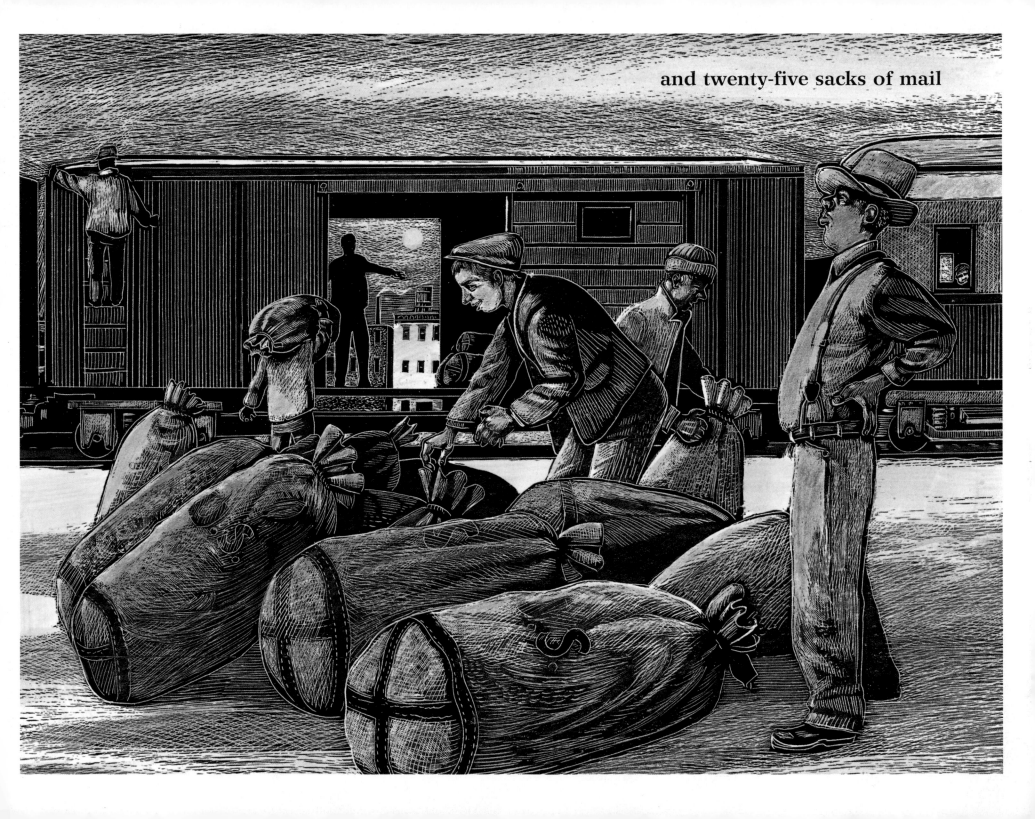

and twenty-five sacks of mail

All along the southbound odyssey
    The train pulls out of Kankakee
and rolls along past houses, farms, and fields

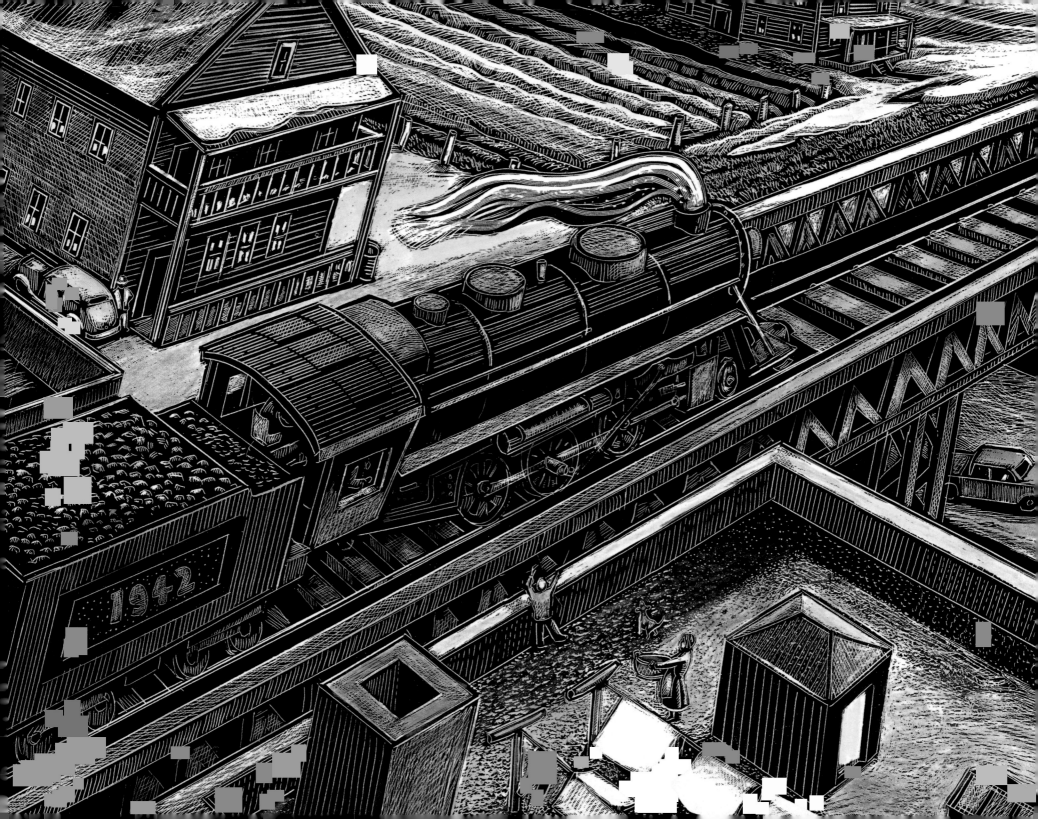

Passing towns that have no name

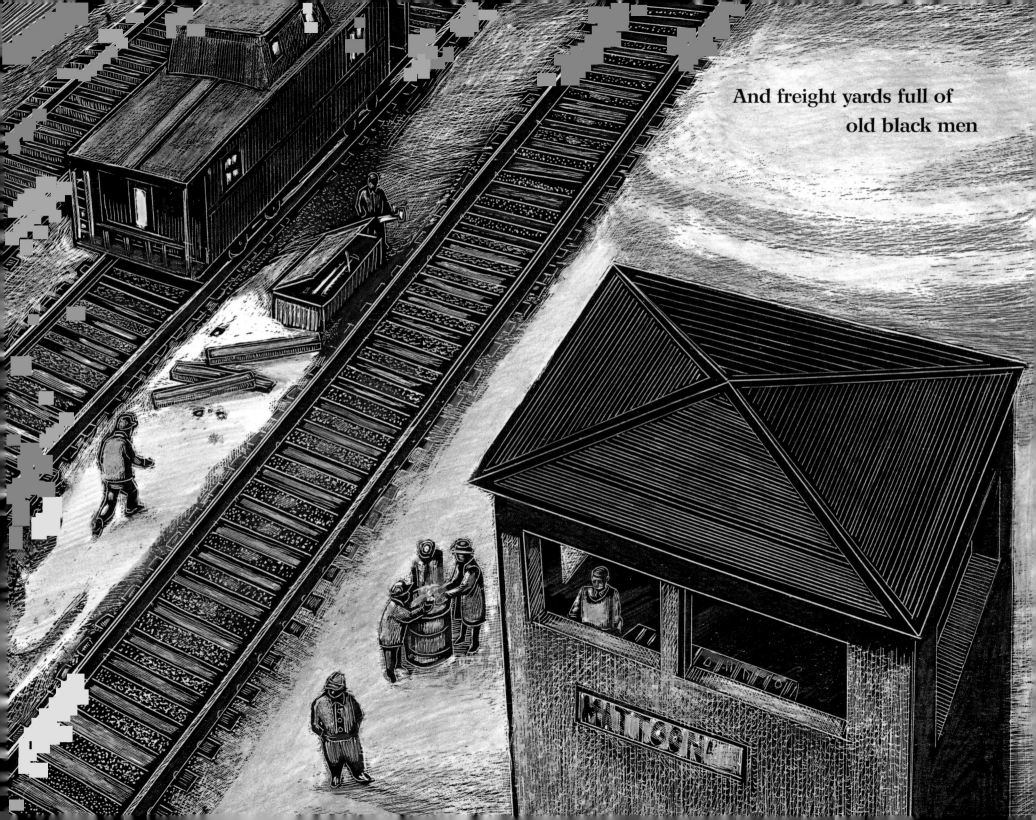

And freight yards full of
old black men

And the graveyards of the rusted automobiles

Deal card games with the old men in the club car
Penny a point, ain't no one keeping score

Pass the paper bag that holds the bottle

Feel the wheels grumbling 'neath the floor

And the sons of Pullman porters

Mothers with their babes asleep
are rocking to the gentle beat

And the rhythm of the rails is all they feel

Nighttime on the City of New Orleans
Changing cars in Memphis, Tennessee

Halfway home, we'll be there by morning
Through the Mississippi darkness rolling down to the sea

But all the towns and people seem to fade into a bad dream
And the steel rail still ain't heard the news

Good morning, America, how are you?
Say, don't you know me, I'm your native son
I'm the train they call the City of New Orleans
I'll be gone five hundred miles when the day is done